For my son, Tim, who is deciding
what to do with the rest of his life.

First published in Great Britain by Andersen Press Ltd in 1998
First published in Picture Lions in 2000.
1 3 5 7 9 10 8 6 4 2
ISBN: 0 00 6646557

Picture Lions is an imprint of the Children's Division,
part of HarperCollins Publishers Ltd,
77–85 Fulham Palace Road, Hammersmith, London W6 8JB.
The HarperCollins website address is:
www.fireandwater.com

Printed in Hong Kong

No animals were hurt in the making of this book. Oh, except Mister Wolf, of course.

Hmm...

Colin McNaughton

Hmm...

PictureLions

An Imprint of HarperCollinsPublishers

One fine day...

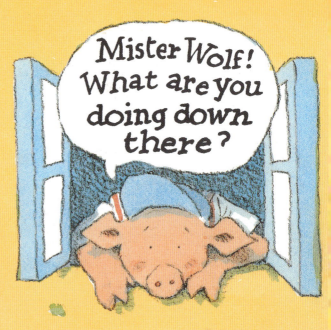

"Well, clever chops," said Mister Wolf. "What sort of job do you suggest?"

"Well," said Preston, "what do you want to be?"

"Hmm..." said Mister Wolf.

"Full-up."

"What are you good at?" said Preston.

"Hmm..." said Mister Wolf.

"Eating pigs."

"And what do you enjoy?" said Preston.

"Hmm..." said Mister Wolf.

"Eating pigs *and* being full-up."

"You could be a footballer," said Preston.

"Hmm..." said Mister Wolf. "I wouldn't mind a shot at that."

"You could be a school teacher," said Preston.

"Hmm..." said Mister Wolf. "I could certainly teach you a lesson or two!"

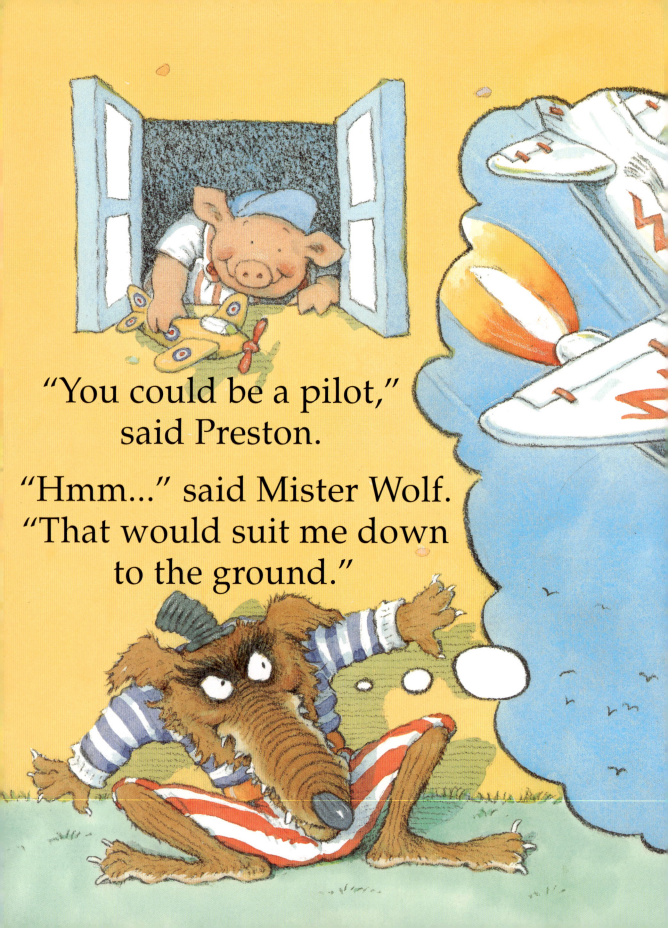

"You could be a pilot,"
said Preston.

"Hmm..." said Mister Wolf.
"That would suit me down
to the ground."

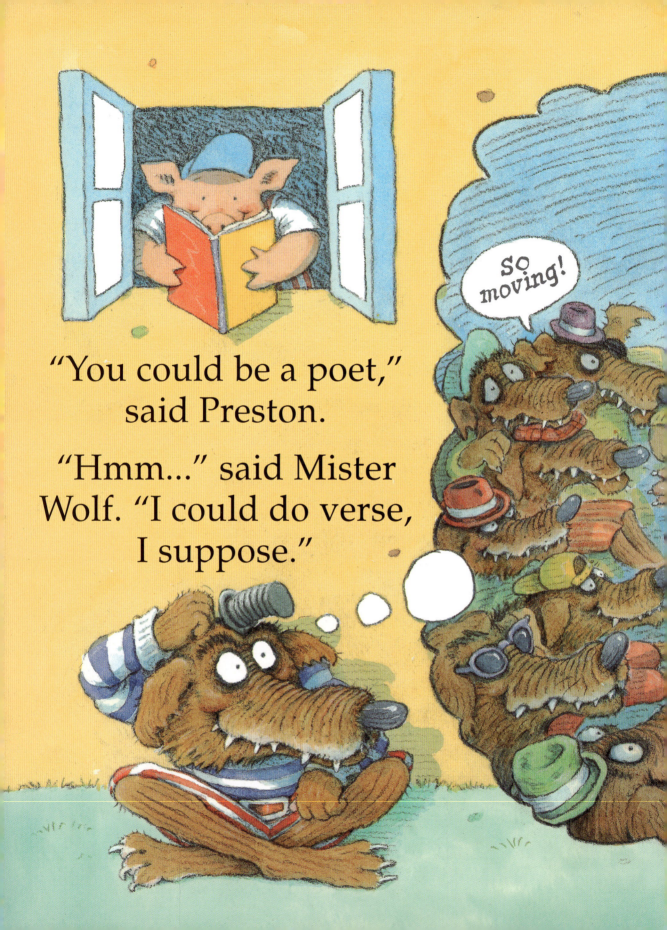

"You could be a poet," said Preston.

"Hmm..." said Mister Wolf. "I could do verse, I suppose."

"You could be a crane driver," said Preston.

"Hmm..." said Mister Wolf. "That's a smashing idea!"

"You could be a sailor," said Preston.

"Hmm..." said Mister Wolf. "I could take that idea on board."

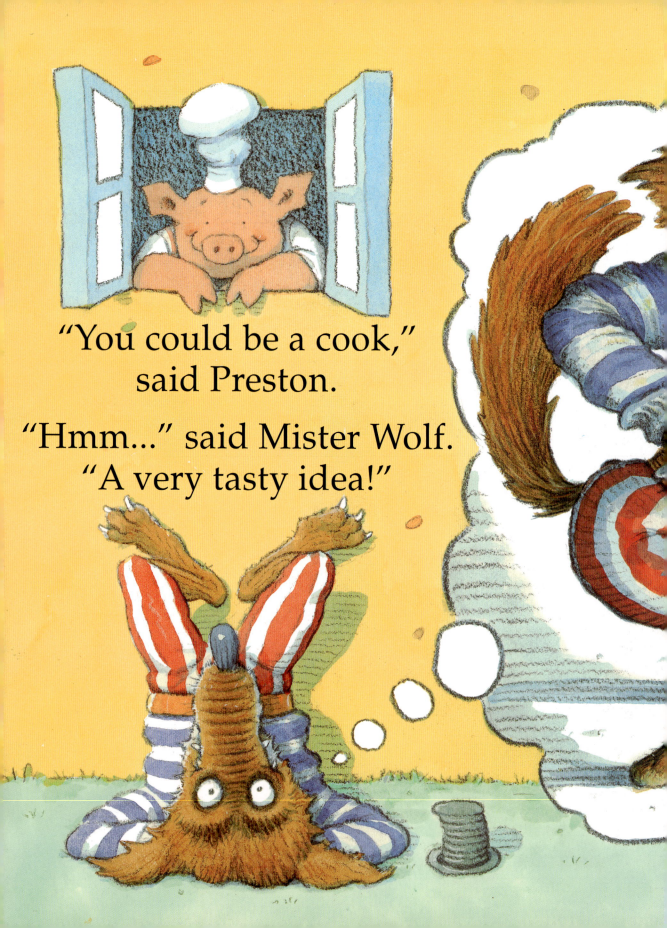

"You could be a cook,"
said Preston.

"Hmm..." said Mister Wolf.
"A very tasty idea!"

"So, Mister Wolf,"
said Preston,
"what do you think?"

"Hmm..." said Mister Wolf.
"It's certainly food
for thought!"

Suddenly!

Preston. Dinner's ready!

Coming mum!

Preston! Have you left that window open?

Sorry mum. I'll close it.

Thanks dad.

Huh! It's all right for some! I have to find my _own_ dinner!

I mean, people don't realize what hard work it is catching pigs! All that scheming and creeping about— all that sneaking around...grumble... .grumble...

COLIN McNAUGHTON was born in Northumberland and had his first book published while he was still at college. He is now one of Britain's most highly acclaimed authors and illustrators of children's books and a winner of many prestigious awards, including the Kurt Maschler award in 1991.

Hmm... is the fifth hilarious book featuring Preston the pig. The first, *Suddenly!*, was shortlisted for both the Smarties and the WH Smith/*SHE* Under-Fives awards. The third book in this series, *Oops!*, won the 1996 Smarties Book Prize in the under-fives category.

"Quite simply the book's a gem."
Bookseller

"The illustrations are a delight.
This is a super book."
School Librarian

*Look out for the fantastic
lift-the-flap book featuring Preston
and friends, to be published in
Collins Picture Lions in 2001.*

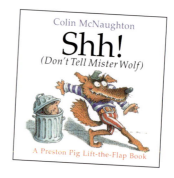